You and Your Pet
Hamster and Gerbil

Jean Coppendale

QED Publishing

Copyright © QED Publishing 2004

First published in the UK in 2004 by
QED Publishing
A division of Quarto Publishing plc
The Fitzpatrick Building
188–194 York Way, London N7 9QP
United Kingdom

A Catalogue record for this book is available from the British Library.

ISBN 1 84538 055 X

Written by Jean Coppendale
Consultant Michaela Miller
Designed by Susi Martin
Editor Gill Munton
All photographs by Jane Burton except
page 18 (vegetables) by Chris Taylor
Picture of Cuddles on page 29 by Adelle Tracy
With many thanks to Adelle Tracey and Jumaane Bant

Creative Director Louise Morley
Editorial Manager Jean Coppendale

Printed and bound in China

Words in **bold**
are explained
on page 32.

Contents

Your first hamster or gerbil

Hamsters and gerbils are lively little animals, and they love to play. Hamsters are nocturnal. This means that they like to sleep during the day and wake up at night.

▼ **Hamsters and gerbils are small and fragile.**

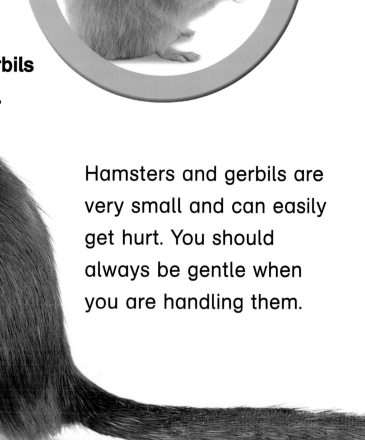

Hamsters and gerbils are very small and can easily get hurt. You should always be gentle when you are handling them.

Hamsters are nocturnal, and do not make good pets for young children as they tend to be asleep when the child wants to play. Hamsters and gerbils are easily hurt if they are dropped, so they may not be suitable pets for children who are boisterous. Children should always be supervised by an adult when they are playing with their hamster or gerbil.

Looking after an animal is your responsibility, not your child's. Before you buy one, try to make sure that he or she is not going to get bored with the hamster or gerbil.

▲ **Hamsters and gerbils usually live for between two to three years.**

Which pet?

Gerbils are very lively and do not like to be alone. It is best to buy two brothers or two sisters and keep them together.

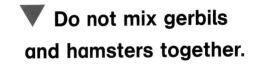
Hamsters like to live alone.

Hamsters sleep during the day and wake up at night, so you will not be able to play with your hamster in the daytime. Do not mix gerbils and hamsters together.

Do not mix gerbils and hamsters together.

Lots of pets

There are many different **breeds** of hamster and gerbil. These have differently coloured fur and different markings.

◀ **Black Mongolian gerbil**

▶ **Agouti Syrian hamster**

▼ **Lilac Mongolian gerbil**

◀ **Black Syrian hamster**

▶ **Albino gerbils**

▲ **Golden Satin Syrian hamster**

Pet shopping list

Your hamster or gerbils will need:

◀ A small cardboard box as a nest filled with shredded white kitchen towel, never use newspaper.

▼ Or you could use hay...

...or wood shavings. Never use cedar or pine.

▼ A cage or a plastic tank

▶ Hamster food or gerbil food

▲ A scoop for cleaning out the tank

◀ A food bowl and a water bottle with a metal spout

Your pet will enjoy some toys

Getting ready

The best home for a hamster or some gerbils is a plastic tank or a wire cage with a solid floor. It should be big enough for your pet to run around in.

Cover the floor with a layer of wood shavings. Add little piles of hay or shredded white kitchen towel so that your pet can make a cosy nest.

▲ **Gerbils will make a sleeping nest from the material you put in their tank.**

▲ **Make sure your hamster's tank or cage has a separate, nest box.**

Parent Points
The tank or cage should measure at least 75cm x 40cm x 40cm – high enough for a hamster or gerbil to be able to stand up on its hind legs – but the bigger the better. Wood is not a suitable material, as these pets would gnaw it. Make sure that the tank is placed away from draughts, as well as direct sunlight, radiators and other forms of heating, and sources of loud noise such as televisions, radios, sound systems or telephones.

Saying hello

When your pet arrives, it may be feeling very scared. Place it gently in its tank or cage, and leave it alone for a couple of hours to get used to its new home.

Do not make any loud noises near it. Talk to it quietly, so that it begins to know your voice.

▲ It will take a few hours for your pet to get used to its new home.

◀ Your pet will soon begin to explore its new home and will like to run up and down ladders in its cage or tank.

Offer your pet a treat, such as a piece of apple. After a couple of days your pet will begin to get used to you and let you cup it in your hand.

Parent Points
Make sure your child knows how to handle the hamster or gerbil before he or she tries to pick it up (see pages 16–17).

Handle with care

Hamsters and gerbils are very small, and a hand swooping down would scare them. Slowly put your closed hand into the tank or cage, and let your pet sniff it. Slowly open your hand, and let your pet climb onto your palm.

▲ **Always use two hands to hold your pet.**

◀ **To pick up your pet, gently scoop it into your palm. Never grab your pet around its body or dangle it by its tail.**

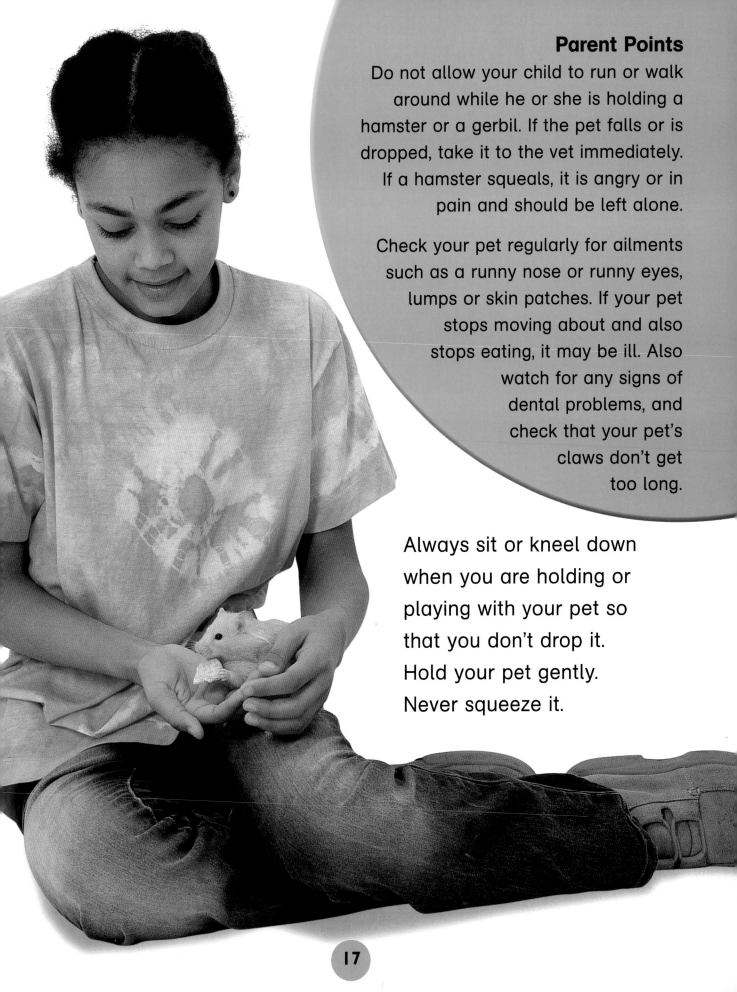

Always sit or kneel down when you are holding or playing with your pet so that you don't drop it. Hold your pet gently. Never squeeze it.

Feeding your pet

◀ **Your pet should always have some food. Buy special hamster or gerbil food from a pet shop or vet.**

▲ **Carrot-shaped wood gnawing block**

Feed your pet a piece of fresh fruit or vegetable every day. Try carrot, apple, celery, broccoli, banana or cucumber.

As a treat, hide a piece of plain biscuit or dry bread in the cage for your pet to find. Never give it sweets or sticky food.

Broccoli

Celery

Make sure your pet has a block of wood to gnaw on. This will help to keep its teeth short and healthy.

Make sure your pet's water bottle always has plenty of clean water in it.

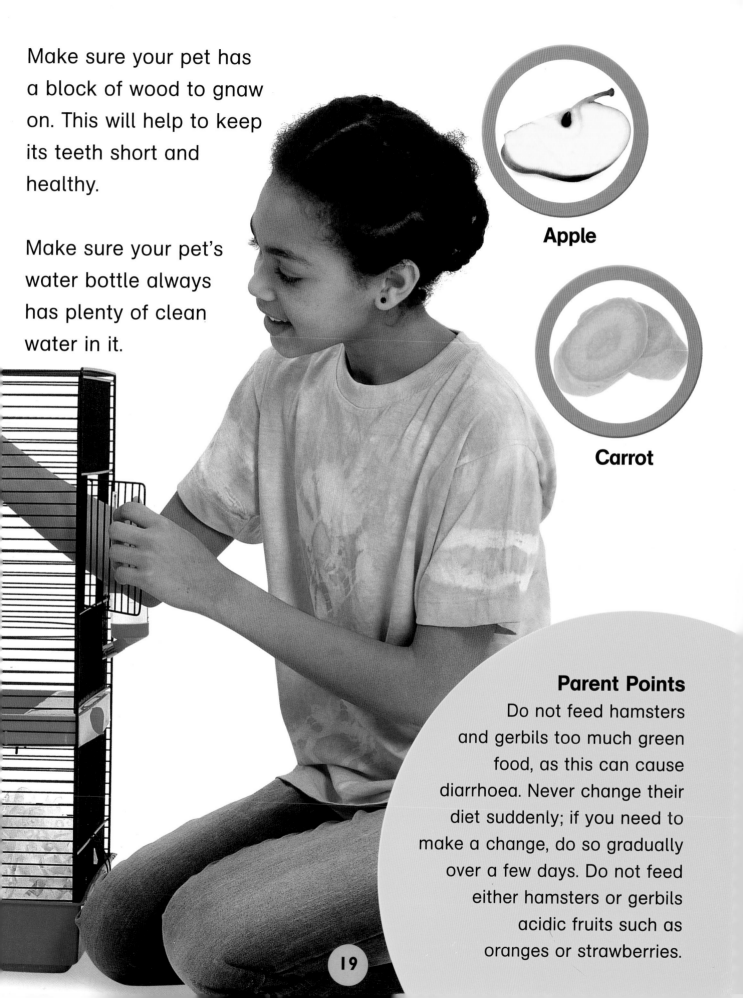

Apple

Carrot

Parent Points

Do not feed hamsters and gerbils too much green food, as this can cause diarrhoea. Never change their diet suddenly; if you need to make a change, do so gradually over a few days. Do not feed either hamsters or gerbils acidic fruits such as oranges or strawberries.

Keep it clean

Your hamster's and gerbils' tank or cage needs to be kept clean. Give your hamster's home a really good clean every week. You should clean out your gerbil every two weeks.

Give the tank or cage a really good clean with a little animal-safe disinfectant. Wipe all the surfaces, and wash the toys.

Once a day, use the scoop to clear out droppings and old bits of food.

Wash the food bowl every day. Clean out the water bottle with a bottle brush once a week.

Always wash your hands after you have cleaned out the tank.

Parent Points
Use animal-safe disinfectant (available from pet shops) for cleaning the tank. Make sure the pet is put somewhere safe while its home is being cleaned.

Your gerbil's life cycle

5

▶ When a female gerbil is about 9 weeks old, she can have babies. Her babies drink her milk. This is called suckling.

◀ At six weeks old, a gerbil is old enough to leave its mother.

4

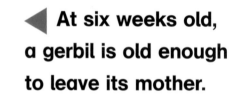

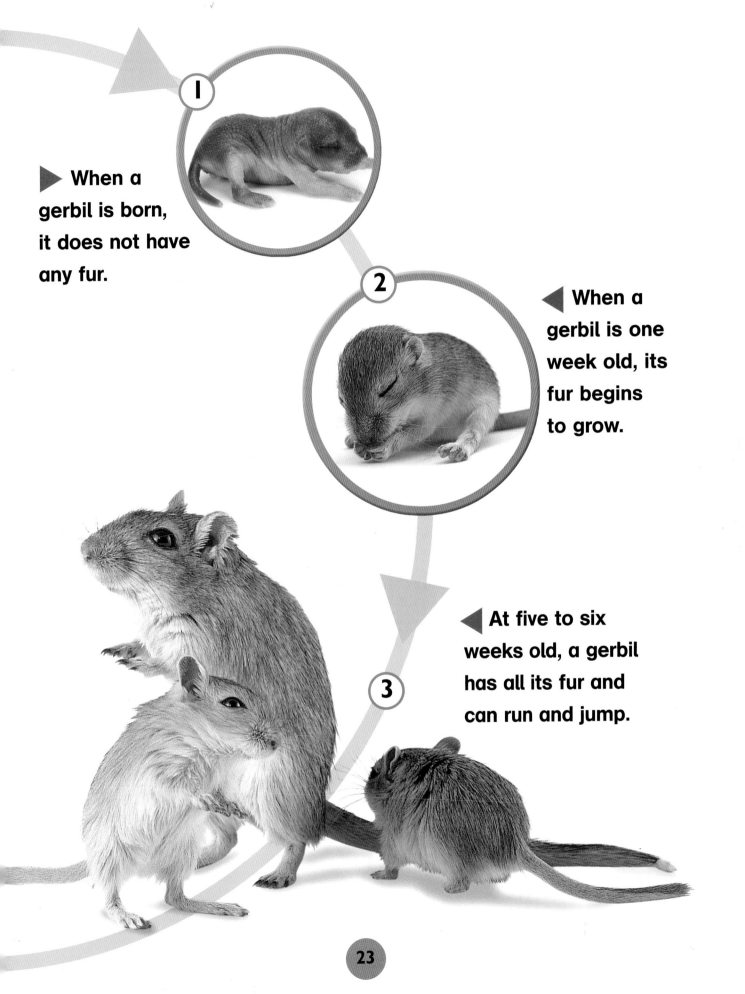

▶ When a gerbil is born, it does not have any fur.

◀ When a gerbil is one week old, its fur begins to grow.

◀ At five to six weeks old, a gerbil has all its fur and can run and jump.

Let's play!

Gerbils and hamsters are very active, so give your pet some toys. Put some cardboard tubes in the tank or cage. Cut holes in a plastic bottle for your pet to explore.

Hide some food for your pet to find.

▼ **Your pet will love to climb in and out of holes.**

▶ As a special treat, buy your pet a play tank. You'll enjoy watching it have fun.

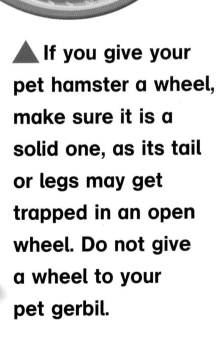

▲ If you give your pet hamster a wheel, make sure it is a solid one, as its tail or legs may get trapped in an open wheel. Do not give a wheel to your pet gerbil.

Parent Points
Hamsters and gerbils should be allowed out of the tank or cage once a day, so that they can get some exercise. Make a playground in a large cardboard box with some toys. Make sure your pet cannot escape into corners, under doors, up chimneys, behind skirting boards or into pieces of furniture, and keep cats and dogs out of the room.

Make a

▼ Make a playground for your pet to exercise in. Use an old cardboard box, old toilet roll tubes and old kitchen roll tubes and cartons.

playground

Saying goodbye

Pets grow older, just as people do. As your pet grows older, it will play less and spend more time sleeping. Don't give it as much food as before, or it will get fat.

My pet Cuddles

◀ If your pet is ill, or appears to be in pain, take it to the vet.

Cuddles last summer

Keep a special scrapbook about your pet

If your pet is very old or ill, it may die. Try not to be too sad, and remember all the fun you had.

You may want to bury your pet in the garden, or you can take it to the vet.

Pet checklist

Read this list, and think about all the points.

✔ **Hamsters and gerbils are not toys.**

✔ **Treat your pet gently – as you would like to be treated yourself.**

✔ **Gerbils and hamsters are very small and can be easily hurt if you are not gentle.**

✔ **How will you treat your pet if it makes you angry?**

✔ **Never shout at your pet, or frighten it.**

✔ **Animals feel pain, just as you do.**

✔ **Will you be happy to clean out your pet's cage or tank every day?**

Parents' checklist

● **You**, not your child, are responsible for the care of the pet.

● Your pet will need someone to look after it every day when you are away from home – this includes feeding, cleaning and exercising.

● Hamsters and gerbils are small pets, and can easily be stepped on – make sure your child is aware of the dangers.

● Exercise wheels are not suitable toys for gerbils as their tails can become trapped.

● Hamsters will bite if they are scared or angry.

● Hamsters should be left to sleep during the day. Don't keep two hamsters together, even if they are from the same litter.

● Never use newspaper in your pet's cage – it is poisonous to both hamsters and gerbils.

● Always supervise pets and children.

● If hamsters get too cold, they may go into hibernation and appear dead. Cup your hamster gently in your hands to warm it up.

Pet words

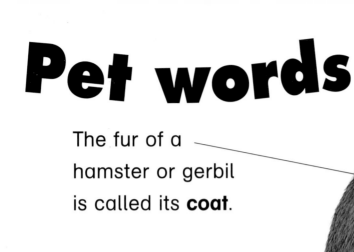

The fur of a hamster or gerbil is called its **coat**.

The long hairs on the face of a hamster or gerbil are called **whiskers**.

A gerbil has a long **tail**.

A hamster has hardly any **tail**.

Hamsters and gerbils have **claws** on their toes.

A **breed** is a special type of hamster or gerbil, such as a Black Mongolian gerbil or Black Syrian hamster.

Index